This book belongs to:

....

The Ghost Orchid has no leaves, just roots that wrap around the trees

SOCIETY OF EXPLORERS

Dear Fiona and David,

It is with very great pleasure that we can confirm the society is willing to fund your trip to find the rare and mysterious ghost orchid. Good luck on your trip and we hope to hear of your success.

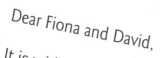

Please find

Ghost Orchids
flower
for just
one or
two weeks

Their locations
are kept
secret to
protect these
rare flowers

Ghost Orchid
flowers
smell fruity,
like apples

POST CARD

FOR
SONNY & TEDDY,
AND EVERY LITTLE
EXPLORER WHO
NOTICES THE
MAGIC ALL
AROUND THEM.

SPECIAL THANKS
TO LIBBY, BECCY
& SUE.

FERRY SERVICE
ROUND TRIP
2 x ADULTS 1 x CHILD
A 0123456

ROUND TRIP
2 x A 1 x C
A 0123456

POST CARD

This paperback edition first published
in 2023 by Andersen Press Ltd.
First published in Great Britain in 2022 by
Andersen Press Ltd., 20 Vauxhall Bridge Road,
London SW1V 2SA, UK.
Vijverlaan 48, 3062 HL Rotterdam, Nederland.
Copyright © Fiona Lumbers 2022.
The right of Fiona Lumbers to be identified as

the author and illustrator of this work has been
asserted by her in accordance with the
Copyright, Designs and Patents Act, 1988.
All rights reserved.
Printed and bound in China.
1 3 5 7 9 10 8 6 4 2
British Library Cataloguing in Publication
Data available. ISBN 978 1 83913 138 7

Fiona Lumbers

Ghost Orchid

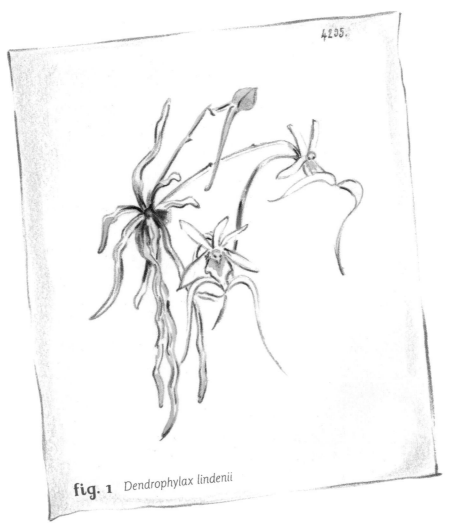

4295.

fig. 1 *Dendrophylax lindenii*

ANDERSEN PRESS

My family are explorers and today we got a special letter. We are being sent on an adventure to find a very special, rare flower called the ghost orchid.

Mum says, *Hurry, Ava, hurry – the ghost orchids will soon be in bloom!*

Dad says, *Hurry, Ava, hurry – pack light, there's not much room.*

They say, *Hurry, Ava, hurry – the ferry's leaving soon.*

When we're on an adventure,
Mum and Dad don't think
about anything else.

What's that light?

Later, Ava, later.

Does it glow all night?

Later, Ava, later.

I can't work out this map.

Later, Mummy, later.

They don't
talk about
anything else.

Ghost orchids often flower for just one week. They're hard to find, never mind photograph.

They bloom in
special, secret places, where
the sunlight and the water are just right.

It's, *Just a little further, Ava,* when I
stop to hear the rustle of wings.

And, *Time to sleep now, Sweetheart,*
when I'm staring up at things.

It's, *Don't do dragging, Ava,* when someone new swings by.

And, *Stop mucking about Ava,* when I copy friends who fly.

It's curious, even though they're explorers, that there's so much Mum and Dad don't notice.

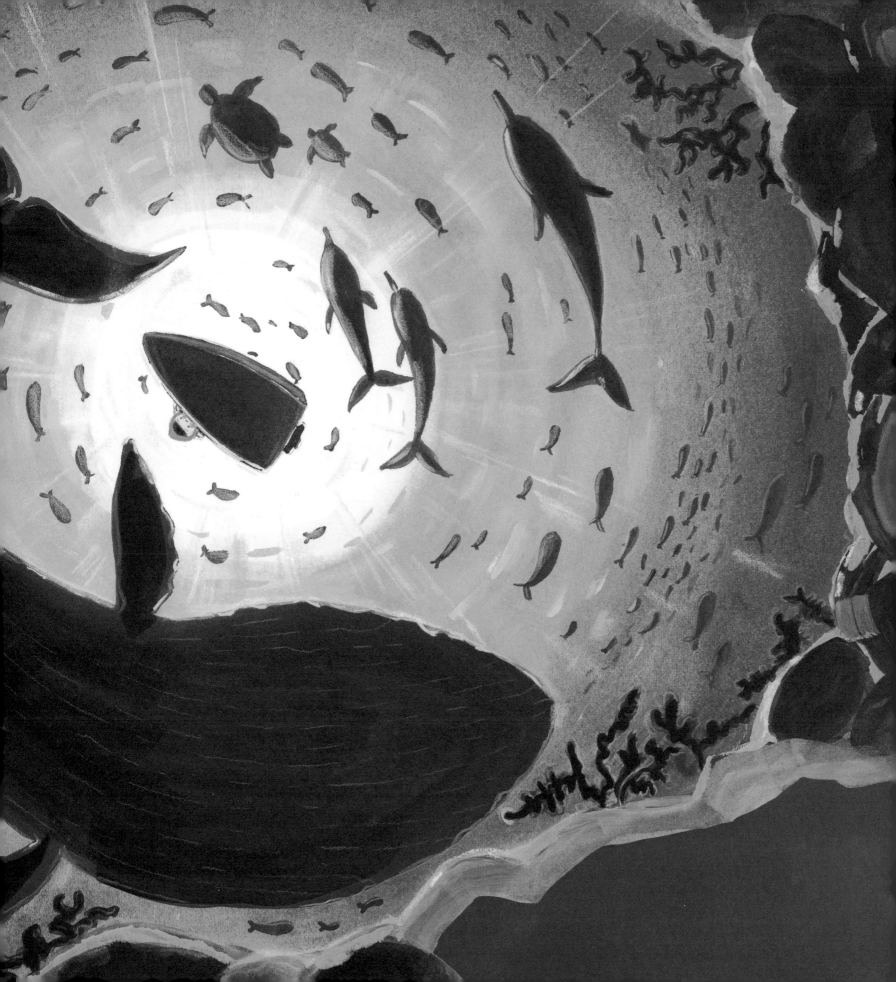

I love every single minute of my trips with Mum and Dad,

but they can get really sad if things don't go to plan.

Oh no, it's withered and gone.

Luckily they've got me. I'm the explorer who notices things
that aren't in the plan. The lights and stars, the rocks that
kiss, the animals, treasures and new friends they miss.

I keep all the memories safe
inside my pack.

And then I see them. "GHOST
ORCHIDS," I shout. "Wow!"
I look right at the here and now,
and special things find me, somehow.

From now on, Mum and Dad say,
We'll all explore the Ava way.

I wonder what will happen on our trip home?
After all, in my family, we are real explorers.